Monsieur Roscoe
On Vacation

Jim Field

At the very top of a very tall building lives
a friendly dog called Monsieur Roscoe.

Bonjour Monsieur Roscoe!

Today is a special day. Monsieur Roscoe and his goldfish, Fry, are going on vacation to visit their friends.

Bonjour, je m'appelle Monsieur Roscoe.
Hello, my name is Mr. Roscoe.

It's time to pack. There are lots of things to remember.
Don't forget your toothbrush, Monsieur Roscoe!

un pantalon
trousers

un short
shorts

un T-shirt
T-shirt

une chemise
shirt

des chaussettes
socks

des lunettes de soleil
sunglasses

des chaussures
shoes

un nounours
teddy bear

un parapluie
umbrella

un slip
underpants

At last, Monsieur Roscoe and Fry are ready to leave.

Have fun, Monsieur Roscoe!

un taxi
taxi

un camion poubelle
garbage truck

un bus
bus

une moto
motorbike

une voiture
car

un vélo
bike

une ambulance
ambulance

The city is big, and the streets are very busy.

Hurry up, Monsieur Roscoe, or you'll miss your train!

ÉPICERIE

COIFFEUR

BOULANGERIE

BOULANGERI

OUVRE

PÂTISSERIE

n fourgon
postal
mail truck

un scooter
scooter

une voiture de police
police car

Monsieur Roscoe and Fry catch the train, just in time.
Phew! That was close!

The train goes into the tunnel . . .

. . . and comes out into the countryside.

Monsieur Roscoe and Fry are going
camping with their friend Eva.
Oh no, it's starting to rain!

Monsieur Roscoe has brought his camping gear, but – oh dear! – he doesn't know how to put up a tent.

une clôture
fence

un camping car
camper

une ombre
shadow

le ronflement
snore

une tente
tent

un feu de camp
campfire

une bûche
log

la lune
moon

une lampe torche
flashlight

une caravane
trailer

un buisson
bush

un barbecue
barbecue

une table de pique-nique
picnic table

des bottes
boots

Luckily, Eva can help.
Where's your teddy, Monsieur Roscoe?

After a night under the stars, it's time to say *au revoir*.

**Soon Monsieur Roscoe and Fry are on a bus,
traveling up into the snowy mountains.**

They catch a lift to the very top of the ski slopes.

It's a long way down from the top of the mountain …
Oh crumbs, Monsieur Roscoe, that's the ski jump!

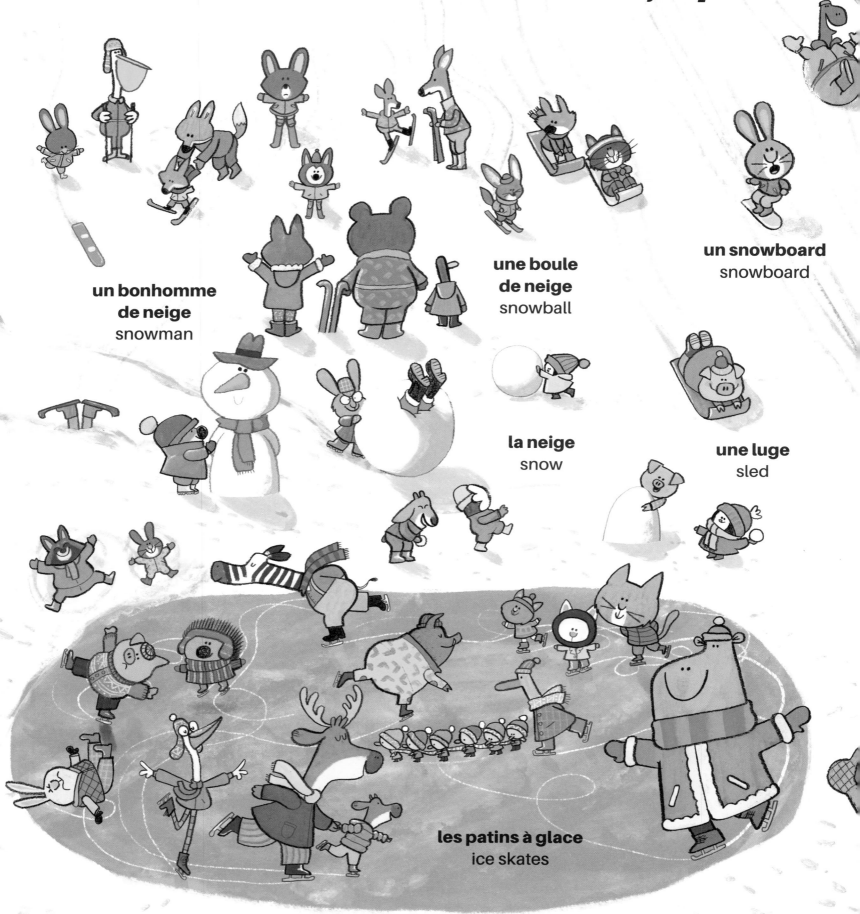

un bonhomme
de neige
snowman

une boule
de neige
snowball

un snowboard
snowboard

la neige
snow

une luge
sled

les patins à glace
ice skates

un bonnet
beanie

la montagne
mountain

des skis
skis

un télésiège
chairlift

des bâtons
de ski
ski poles

des gants
gloves

un saut
à ski
ski jump

10

10

10

10

Wowee!
Stan and the crowd
are very impressed!

Stan would like to take Monsieur Roscoe snowboarding.
But it's time to move on. *Next time, Monsieur Roscoe.*

It's hard work cycling to the lake.

Time for a rest, Monsieur Roscoe?

Monsieur Roscoe and Fry are glad to see their friend Caro. She is going to take them for a trip on her boat!

la forêt
forest

la colline
hill

un voilier
sailboat

une péniche
houseboat

un bateau de pêche
fishing boat

une barque
rowboat

un canoë
canoe

le lac
lake

le paddle
paddleboard

un radeau
raft

la planche à voile
windsurfing

les skis nautiques
water skis

une gondole
gondola

un bateau à moteur
motorboat

Monsieur Roscoe wants to try steering
the boat. But it isn't as easy as it looks...
Watch out, Monsieur Roscoe!

All too soon, it's time to go. Caro helps them find
a big boat to take them on their way…

The next stop is Monsieur Roscoe's favorite place…

…the seaside!

Monsieur Roscoe can't wait to go swimming
with his friends Jojo and Didi.

J'adore la mer !
I love the sea!

Viens jouer !
Come and play!

*Don't forget your goggles,
Monsieur Roscoe!*

Monsieur Roscoe loves splashing in the sea. Everyone is very impressed with his floaty!

un sauveteur
lifeguard

un maillot de bain
swimsuit

un cerf-volant
kite

une serviette
towel

un parasol
umbrella

la plage
beach

la crème solaire
sunscreen

un château de sable
sandcastle

la natation
swimming

le surf
surfing

la mer
sea

des vagues
waves

une bouée
floaty

des raquettes
racquets

Monsieur Roscoe and Fry have had a wonderful time at the beach, but there is still one more friend to visit.

They take a taxi to a pretty little village.

Look where you're going, Monsieur Roscoe!

Monsieur Roscoe and Dougal order TWO ice creams each, and a big fruity drink for Fry.

du pain
bread

de l'eau
water

un café
coffee

une salade
salad

un jus
juice

une glace
ice cream

un burger
burger

des olives
olives

une chaise
chair

du fromage
cheese

un gâteau
cake

des frites
French fries

une table
table

des bananes
bananas

This is the life, Monsieur Roscoe!

What a wonderful trip! But now, it's time to go home.

Monsieur Roscoe and Fry have had great fun with all of their friends.

Don't worry, Monsieur Roscoe, you'll see them again soon.

After a long journey, Monsieur Roscoe and
Fry make it back home to the city.

Monsieur Roscoe has had a fantastic vacation.
But it's good to be back home.
Bonne nuit Monsieur Roscoe.
Bonne nuit Fry.

Bonne nuit everybody.

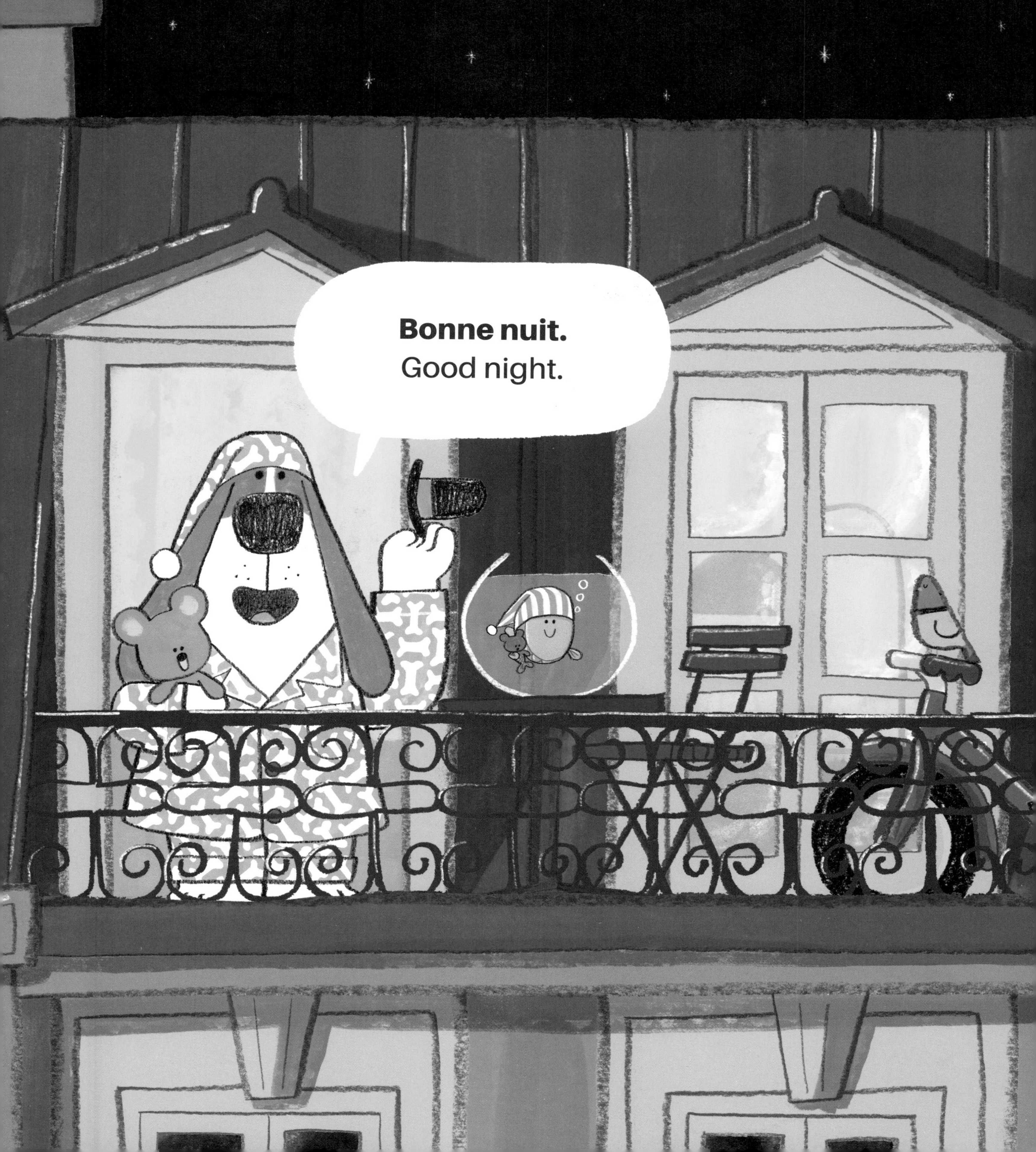

Monsieur Roscoe and Fry hope you've had fun with them on vacation. Can you spot the following items in the book?

IN THE CITY

- **orange car**
  une voiture orange
- **hairdresser**
  un coiffeur
- **pigeon**
  un pigeon

ON THE SLOPES

- **tiger**
  un tigre
- **6 yellow ducklings**
  6 canetons jaunes
- **zebra**
  un zèbre

AT THE SEASIDE

- **beach ball**
  un ballon de plage
- **surfer**
  un surfeur
- **6 crabs**
  6 crabes

ON THE CAMPSITE

- **pink tent**
  une tente rose
- **guitar**
  une guitare
- **bird**
  un oiseau

ON THE LAKE

- **2 fishermen**
  2 pêcheurs
- **4 fish**
  4 poissons
- **mouse**
  une souris

AT THE CAFÉ

- **baby leopard**
  un bébé léopard
- **pizza**
  une pizza
- **hen**
  une poule

First American Edition 2020
Kane Miller, A Division of EDC Publishing

Copyright © Jim Field 2020
The moral rights of the author and illustrator have been asserted.
First published in Great Britain in 2020 by Hodder and Stoughton,
an imprint of Hachette Children's Group, An Hachette UK Company.

All rights reserved. For information contact:
Kane Miller, A Division of EDC Publishing
www.kanemiller.com
www.usbornebooksandmore.com
Library of Congress Control Number: 2019957556
10 9 8 7 6 5 4 3 2
Printed and bound in China
ISBN: 978-1-68464-180-2

To "mon amour" Sandy. Thanks to your ideas, patience, support, encouragement and French!
Without you, this book would never have existed. Merci beaucoup ma chérie!